Snapshots

Alain Robbe-Grillet was born in 1922 in Brest, France. He worked as an agronomist from 1945 to 1951 in Paris, Africa, and the Antilles. His first novel, *The Erasers,* appeared in 1953 and marked the beginning of a literary career which astonished and enraged the critics. As his later works appeared—*The Voyeur* (1955), *Jealousy* (1957), *In the Labyrinth* (1959), and *La Maison de Rendez-vous* (1965)—his importance became apparent, and he is now the chief spokesman for the *nouveau roman* which has caused much discussion and controversy. Robbe-Grillet's own theories of the novel appear in his essays on fiction, *For a New Novel,* one of the most intriguing works of criticism to be published in recent years.

Robbe-Grillet is also the author of the film *Last Year at Marienbad,* and author and director of *L'Immortelle, Trans-Europ Express,* and *L'Homme qui Ment.*

SNAPSHOTS

by Alain Robbe-Grillet

Translated by Bruce Morrissette
GROVE PRESS, INC., NEW YORK

Contents

THREE REFLECTED VISIONS

The Dressmaker's Dummy

The coffeepot is on the table.

It is a four-legged round table, covered with a waxy oilcloth patterned in red and gray squares against a neutral background of yellowish white that may have been formerly ivory colored—or white. In the center, a square ceramic tile serves as a protective base; its design is entirely hidden, or at least made unrecognizable, by the coffeepot placed upon it.

The coffeepot is made of brown earthenware. It consists of a sphere topped by a cylindrical filter holder with a mushroom-shaped lid. The spout is an S with flattened curves, widening out slightly at the base. The handle has, perhaps, the shape of an ear, or rather of the outer fold of an ear; but it would be a misshapen ear, too circular and lacking a lobe, which would thus resemble a "pitcher handle." The spout, the handle, and the mushroom lid are of a creamy color. The rest is of a very light, smooth brown, and shiny.

There is nothing on the table except the waxy tablecloth, the ceramic base, and the coffeepot.

On the right, in front of the window, stands the dressmaker's dummy.

Behind the table, the space above the mantel holds a large rectangular mirror in which may be seen half of the window (the right half) and, on the left (that is, on the right side of the window), the reflection of the wardrobe with its mirror front. In the wardrobe mirror the window may again be seen, in its entirety now, and unreversed (that is, the right French pane on the right and the left one on the left).

Thus there are, above the mantel, three half-sections of window one after another, with an almost unresolved continuity, and which are, in turn (from left to right): one left section unreversed, one right section unreversed, and one right section reversed. Since the wardrobe stands in the corner of the room and extends to the outer edge of the window, the two right half-sections of the latter are seen separated only by a narrow vertical piece of wardrobe, which might be the wood separating the two French window sections (the right upright edge of the left side joined to the left edge of the right side). The three window sections, above the half-curtains, give a view of the leafless trees in the garden.

In this way, the window takes up the entire surface of the mirror, except for the upper portion, in which can be seen a strip of ceiling and the top of the mirrored wardrobe.

In the mirror above the mantel may be seen two other dressmaker's dummies: one in front of the first window section, the narrowest, at the far left, and the other in front of the third section (the one farthest to the right). Neither one is seen straight on; the one on the right has its right side facing the view; the one on the left, slightly smaller, reveals its left side. But it is difficult to be certain of this on first glance, because the two reflections are facing in the same direction and as a consequence both seem to be turned so that the same side shows—the left side, probably.

The three dummies stand in a line. The middle one, whose size is intermediate between that of the two others, occupies the right side of the mirror, in exactly the same direction as the coffeepot standing on the table.

In the spherical surface of the coffeepot is a shiny, distorted reflection of the window, a sort of four-sided figure whose sides form the arcs of a circle. The line of the wooden uprights between the two window sections widens abruptly at the bottom into a vague spot. This is, no doubt, the shadow of the dressmaker's dummy.

The room is quite bright, since the window is unusually wide, even though it has only two sections.

A good smell of hot coffee rises from the pot on the table.

The dressmaker's dummy is no longer in its accustomed spot: it is normally placed in the corner by the window, opposite the mirrored wardrobe. The wardrobe has been placed in its position to help with the fittings.

The design on the ceramic tile base is the picture of an owl, with two large, somewhat frightening eyes. But, for the moment, it cannot be made out, because of the coffeepot.

The Replacement

The schoolboy stepped slightly backward and looked up toward the lowest branches. Then he took a step forward, to try to reach a branch which seemed within his grasp; he stood on tiptoes and stretched his hand as high as he could, but failed to reach it. After several fruitless efforts, he apparently gave up. He lowered his arm and merely continued to stare at something among the leaves.

Next he returned to the foot of the tree, where he took up the same position as before: his knees bent slightly, the top of his body twisted to the right, and his head bent over toward his shoulder. He still held his book satchel in his left hand. It was impossible to see the other hand, with which he was no doubt supporting himself against the tree, or his face, which was almost glued to the bark of the tree, as if to scrutinize minutely some detail about a yard and a half above the ground.

The boy had again paused in his reading aloud, but this time there must have been a period, perhaps even an indentation, and he gave the impression that he was making an effort to indicate the end of the paragraph. The schoolboy straightened up to inspect the bark of the tree higher up.

Whispers could be heard in the classroom. The schoolmaster turned his head and noticed that most of the pupils were looking up, instead of following the oral reading in their books; even the one reading aloud kept looking toward the teacher's desk with a vaguely questioning, or fearful, expression. The teacher said severely:

"What are you waiting for?"

The faces were all lowered silently and the boy began again, with the same studious voice, expressionless and a bit too slow, that gave each word equal emphasis and spaced it evenly from the next:

"Therefore, that evening, Joseph de Hagen, one of Philippe's lieutenants, went to the Archbishop's palace on the pretext of paying a courtesy call. As previously stated the two brothers . . ."

On the other side of the street, the schoolboy peered again at the leaves on the low branches. The teacher slapped on the desk with the flat of his hand:

"As previously stated, *comma*, the two brothers . . ."

Searching out the passage in his own book, he read aloud, exaggerating the punctuation:

"Start at: 'As previously stated, the two brothers were already there, so that they might, if need be, protect themselves with this alibi . . .' and pay attention to what you are reading."

"As previously stated, the two brothers were already there, so that they might, if need be, protect themselves with this alibi—a suspect alibi in truth, but the best available to them at this juncture—without allowing their mistrustful cousin . . ."

The monotonous voice stopped abruptly, in the middle of the sentence. The other pupils, already raising their eyes toward the paper puppet hanging on the wall, immediately returned to their books. The teacher turned his glance from the window back to the boy who was reading aloud, on the opposite side of the room, in the first row near the door.

"All right, go on! There isn't any period there. You don't seem to understand what you are reading!"

The boy looked at the teacher, and behind him, slightly to the right, the puppet made of white paper.

"Do you understand, or not?"

"Yes," said the boy without much conviction.

"Yes, *sir*," the teacher corrected him.

"Yes, sir," the boy repeated.

The teacher looked at the printed text and asked:

"What does the word 'alibi' mean to you?"

The boy looked at the puppet cut out of paper, then at the blank wall, straight in front of him, then at the book lying on his desk; and then again at the wall, for almost a full minute.

"Well?"

"I don't know, sir," said the boy.

The teacher slowly looked over the other pupils in the class. One boy raised his hand, near the window in back. The teacher pointed at him, and the boy stood up alongside his bench:

"It's to make people think they were there, sir."

"Just what do you mean? Who are *they*?"

"The two brothers, sir."

"Where did they want people to think they were?"

"At the Archbishop's, sir."

"And where were they really?"

The boy thought for a moment before answering.

"But they were really there, sir, only they wanted to go somewhere else and make people think they were still there."

Late at night, hidden under black masks and wrapped in huge capes, the two brothers slid down a long rope ladder into a small, deserted street.

The teacher nodded slightly a couple of times, as if he were giving his halfhearted approval. After several seconds, he said: "Right."

"Now you will summarize for us the whole reading passage, for the benefit of your friends who may not have understood."

The boy looked out the window. Then he glanced down at his book, then up again toward the teacher's desk.

"Where should I start, sir?"

"Start at the beginning of the chapter."

Without sitting down, the boy leafed through the pages of his book and, after a short silence, began to summarize the conspiracy of Philippe de Cobourg. In spite of frequent stops and starts, he did it almost coherently. On the other hand, he stressed unduly a number of secondary matters, while hardly mentioning, or even omitting, certain crucial events. As, moreover, he was disposed to dwell on actions rather than on their political motives, it would have been extremely difficult for an uninformed listener to puzzle out the reasons for the episode or the connections between the various events described, or between the different people involved. The teacher allowed his glance to travel gradually along the windows. The schoolboy had returned to the spot below the lowest tree branch; he had put his satchel at the foot of the tree and was jumping up and down, stretching one arm upward. Seeing that all his attempts were in vain, he again stood motionless, staring at the inaccessible leaves. Philippe de Cobourg had set up camp with his mercenaries on the banks of the Neckar. The pupils, who were no longer required to follow the printed text, had all raised their heads and were silently staring at the paper puppet hanging on the wall. He had no hands or feet, but only four crudely cut-out limbs and a round head, oversized, through which ran the supporting thread. Several inches higher, at the other end of the thread, could be seen the little ball of chewed-up blotting paper that held it on the wall.

But the boy who was reciting was losing his way among wholly insignificant details, so that the teacher finally stopped him:

"That's enough," he said, "we know enough about that. Sit down and we will take up the reading again at the top of the page: 'But Philippe and his followers . . .' "

The whole class, as one, leaned over the desks, and a new reader began, in a voice as devoid of expression as his classmate's, although conscientiously indicating the commas and the periods:

"But Philippe and his followers were not of this opinion. If the majority of the Diet—or even only the barons' party—were to renounce in this manner the prerogatives accorded to them, to him as well as to them, as a result of the invaluable assistance they had given to the Archduke's cause at the time of the uprising, they would be henceforth unable, either they or he, to demand the indictment of any new suspect, or the suspension without trial of his manorial rights. It was absolutely essential that these negotiations, which seemed to him to have begun so inauspiciously for his own cause, be broken off before the fateful date. Therefore, that evening, Joseph de Hagen, one of Philippe's lieutenants, went to the Archbishop's palace on the pretext of paying a courtesy call. As previously stated, the two brothers were already there . . ."

The faces remained dutifully leaning over the desks. The teacher looked at the window. The schoolboy was leaning against the tree, absorbed in his examination of the bark. He crouched down slowly, as if to follow a line running down the trunk—on the side not visible from the school windows. About a yard and a half above the ground, his movement stopped and he tilted his head to one side, in the same position he had formerly occupied. One by one, the faces in the classroom looked up.

The pupils looked at the teacher, then at the windows. But the bottom panes were of frosted glass, and, above, they could see only the treetops and the sky. Not a fly or a butterfly appeared on the windowpanes. Soon all eyes were again fixed on the white paper cutout of a man.

The Wrong Direction

The rainwater has accumulated in the hollow of a shallow depression, forming among the trees a wide pond, roughly circular in shape, some ten yards in diameter. Round about, the earth is black, without the slightest trace of vegetation between the high, straight trunks. There is neither brush nor shrubs in this part of the woods. The ground is covered only with a uniform, feltlike layer made up of twigs and leaves reduced to their veins, from which a few patches of moss protrude slightly in spots, half decomposed. High above the tree trunks, the bare branches stand out sharply against the sky.

The water is transparent, though brownish in color. Bits of debris fallen from the trees—small branches, empty seed pods, pieces of bark—have lain at the bottom of the shallow pond, steeping there since the start of winter. But none of these fragments is light enough to float, to rise and break the surface, which is everywhere uniform and shiny. There is not the slightest breath of air to ruffle this immobility.

The sky has cleared. It is the end of the day. The sun is low, to the left, behind the tree trunks. Its shallowly slanting rays create, over the entire surface of the pond, narrow luminous bands alternating with wider dark bands.

Parallel to these strips, a row of thick trees runs along the water's edge, on the opposite bank; perfect cylinders, vertical, with no low branches, they run downward in a very brilliant reflection of much greater contrast than the real subject—which by comparison seems vague, even somewhat out of focus. In the black water, the symmetrical trunks shine as if varnished. A line of light emphasizes their outlines on the sides turned toward the setting sun.

Yet this admirable landscape is not only inverted, but also discontinuous. The hatching of the sun's rays over the surface of the mirror cuts through the picture with brighter lines, equally spaced and perpendicular to the reflected tree trunks; it is as if the view there was veiled by intense lighting, revealing innumerable particles suspended in the thin top layer of water. Only the shadowed zones, where these particles are invisible, are strikingly brilliant. Thus each tree trunk is cut off, at more or less equal intervals, by a series of uncertain rings (which nevertheless suggest their real models), giving this part of the "deep down" woods a checkered appearance.

Within a hand's grasp, close to the south edge of the pond, the reflected branches join with old, submerged leaves, reddish but still whole, whose intact lacework stands out against the muddy bottom—oak leaves.

Someone, walking noiselessly on the mulchy carpet of the woods, has appeared on the right, moving toward the water. He comes up to the edge and stops. Since the sun is shining directly into his eyes, he has to step to one side to shield his glance.

He then perceives the banded surface of the pond. But, for him, the reflections of the tree trunks merge with their shadows—at least partially, since the trees directly in front of him are not perfectly straight. Moreover, the sunlight prevents him from distinguishing anything clearly. And there are probably no oak leaves at his feet.

This was, then, the end of his walk. Or does he, only now, observe that he has gone in the wrong direction? After a few hesitant glances around, he turns back to the east through the woods, again walking silently, following the path that he had taken to reach this spot.

Once more the scene is empty. On the left, the sun is still at the same height; the light is unchanged. Opposite, the straight, smooth tree trunks are still reflected in the unwrinkled water, perpendicular to the rays of the sunset.

Deep in the shadowed zones shine the sectioned reflections of the columns, upside down and black, washed miraculously clean.

(1954)

THE WAY BACK

Once beyond the line of rocks that had, until then, blocked our view, we saw the mainland again: the hill with the pine woods, the two small white houses, and the gradual slope down which we had walked. We had completed the circle of the island.

And yet, if we could easily recognize the landscape on the mainland, such was not the case for the narrow stretch of water that separated us from it or, even worse, for the shore where we now were. It took us several minutes, then, to realize fully that our way was cut off.

We should have known it at the first glance. The roadway, cut out of the hillside, went down parallel to the shoreline and, at the level of the coarse sand beach, made a sudden bend to the right, to join a sort of stone jetty, wide enough to allow a car to pass, and which permitted one to cross the strait on foot at low tide. At the bend was a high embankment supported by a retaining wall, straight toward which the road ran; seen from the spot where we were, this embankment hid from view the beginning of the jetty. At present, the rest of it was covered with water. It was the change of viewpoint that had puzzled us momentarily: now we were on the island, and then too, we had approached from the opposite direction, walking toward the north, while the end of the road lies toward the south.

From the top of the hill, just after rounding the turn marked by three or four pine trees standing apart from the little woods, one can see straight ahead down the road as far as the jetty, with the arm of the sea to the right, and the island, which is not yet entirely an island. The water, calm as the water in a pond, almost comes over the stone roadway, whose smooth brown surface has the same worn look as that of the nearby rocks. Delicate mossy algae, half bleached by the sun, stain the roadway with greenish spots—the proof that it is subjected to frequent, prolonged immersions. At the other end of the jetty, as on this side, the paved surface rises imperceptibly to meet the dirt road that cuts across the little island; but, on that shore, the road stays quite flat afterward, and meets the jetty at an almost insignificant angle. Although there is no embankment to justify its presence, a retaining wall—symmetrical to the one on this shore—nevertheless protects the left side of the road, from the beginning of the slope to the upper limit of the sand beach—where beach stones of various sizes give way to brush underwood. On the island the vegetation seems even more desiccated than the dusty, yellowed plants that lie about us here.

We go down the road cut out of the hillside, toward

the jetty. Two fishermen's houses face the road on the left; the front of each is newly covered with rough plaster and freshly whitewashed; the only building stones still visible are those round the openings—a low doorway and one small, square window. Windows and doors are closed, and the glass panes masked by wooden shutters without slats, painted a dazzling blue.

Lower down, the edge of the road, cut out of the soil of the hillside, reveals a vertical wall of yellow clay, as high as a man, interrupted here and there by bands of shale rock bristling with sharp-edged broken protrusions; an irregular hedge of thorny brambles and whitethorn runs along the top, cutting off one's view in the direction of the moor and the pine woods. On our right, however, the roadway is bordered only by a narrow embankment, no higher than one or two steps of a stairway, so that one's glance clears it directly, falling upon the rocks of the beach, the motionless water of the strait, the stone jetty, and the little island.

The water almost reaches the level of the stone roadway. We shall have to act quickly. A few more strides and we have completed our descent.

The jetty makes a right angle with the road, which runs abruptly into a wall of yellow earth, triangular in shape, marking the end of the cut made into the side of the hill; its base is protected by a retaining wall that stretches to the right considerably beyond the point of the triangle, alongside the stone pavement, forming a kind of incipient parapet. But it comes to an end after several yards, just as the slope diminishes at the junction with the middle section of the jetty— horizontal and polished smooth by the sea.

Having reached this point, we hesitate to go farther. We look at the island, in front of us, trying to estimate how long it will take to circle it. Of course there is the dirt road that cuts across it, but to take that would scarcely be worth the trouble. We look at the island in front of us and, down by our feet, the stones of the roadway over the jetty, covered here and there by half-dried-up greenish algae. The water almost reaches the level of the algae spots. It is as calm as that of a pond. One cannot see it rising: but one feels that it is, because of the lines of dust that move slowly on its surface between the tufts of sea wrack.

"We won't be able to get back," says Franz.

The island, seen at close range and from the water's level, seems much higher than before—much larger, too. Again we look at the little gray lines that move forward with slow regularity, twisting into spirals among the clumps of seaweed. Legrand says:

"It's not rising so fast."

"All right then, let's hurry."

We set out walking rapidly. But as soon as we have crossed the strait, we leave the roadbed and climb down toward the right to the beach that forms the shore of the island, continuing along the seashore; there the uneven footing, strewn with rocks and holes, makes walking more difficult—and much slower than we had counted on.

Once having set out on this shoreline path, we are unwilling to go back. As we progress, however, the rocks become larger and more numerous. Several times we are obliged to climb over real barriers, stretching so far out into the sea that we cannot go around them.

Elsewhere we have to cross relatively flat places that cause us to lose even more time, since the flat stones are covered with slippery algae. Franz repeats that we shall not be able to get back across the water. Actually it is impossible to know with certainty how fast the water is rising, because we haven't time to stop to observe any change in level. It may even be slack tide.

It is equally difficult to determine what fraction of the whole circuit of the island we have already covered, for outcroppings of land constantly block our view, and one indentation of the coast follows another without constituting the least landmark. Besides, our concern over not losing a single minute over this difficult terrain occupies our entire attention—and the wider landscape disappears, leaving us aware instead of intruding fragments: a water hole to be avoided, a series of loose rocks, a pile of kelp concealing almost any danger, a large rock that must be scaled, another hole surrounded by viscous algae, mud-colored sand which sinks deep beneath our feet—as if to hold them fast.

Finally, after a last line of rocks, which for some time had blocked our view, we saw the mainland again, the hill with the pine woods, the two small white houses and the gradual slope down which we had walked.

At first we did not realize where the jetty was. Between us and the mainland coastline stretched only an arm of the sea whose waters gushed wildly by, toward our right, swirling at various points in rapids and eddies. The shoreline of the island itself seemed changed: now it was a blackish strand, whose visibly horizontal surface shone with innumerable shallow pools of water, at most an inch or two in depth. Beside a short, wooden wharf a rowboat was moored.

The path that led down to the beach at this point did not resemble the dirt road that we remembered. We had not noticed, earlier, the presence of a rowboat. As for the wharf that served for boarding the boat, it had nothing in common with the stone jetty that we had taken on the way over.

It took us several minutes to discover, thirty yards farther on, the two retaining walls that formed, at each end of the passage over the jetty, an incipient parapet. The stone pavement in between had disappeared. The water rushed over it in a milky torrent. The tilted ramps at each end of the jetty no doubt still emerged from the water, but the two low walls were enough to hide these from view. Nor could we see the low point where the road made a right angle, behind the embankment, as it joined the stones of the roadbed over the jetty. Once again we look down at our feet and see the lines of dust rising with slow regularity and twisting into spirals among the clumps of seaweed.

But apart from this almost imperceptible movement on the surface, the water is as calm as that of a pond. Yet it has already come close to the level of the jetty, while on the other side it is still a foot below. It is true that the sea rises much faster in the indentation nearest the entrance of the gulf. When the obstacle interposed by the jetty is overcome, the sudden drop in the water level must produce a current strong enough to make any crossing immediately impossible.

"We won't be able to get back," says Franz.

It was Franz who spoke first.

"I told you we wouldn't be able to get back."

No one answered him. We had reached a point beyond the little jetty; it was obviously useless to jump over the low retaining wall to try to cross on the stone roadway—not because the water was already too deep there, but because the strength of the current would have knocked us over at once and washed us away. Up close, one could clearly see the drop in water level from one side of the jetty to the other: toward the sea, the water was smooth and looked quite motionless; then, at the jetty, it suddenly curved downward, between the two shores, in the form of a cylinder, with no more than an occasional ripple, in such a regular flow that in spite of its velocity it seemed to be without motion—as if caught in a fragile pause in its movement, at some instantaneous moment captured by a photograph, such as that showing a pebble about to break the quiet surface of a pool, frozen in its fall at a point an inch or two above the surface.

Only beyond the smooth cylinder appeared the beginning of the series of turbulent swells and whirlpools whose force was plainly revealed by the whitish color of the water. Yet even there the disturbance had a kind of fixed disorder, in which crests and low swirls remained constantly at the same places, retaining the same form, so that they seemed frozen solid. All this violence of water, in fact, was not so very different from the pattern—scarcely more deceitful—of the little gray lines among the tufts of seaweed, which our conversation, interrupted by pauses, attempts to drive away:

"We won't be able to get back."

"It's not rising so fast."

"All right then, let's hurry."

"What do you expect to find on the other side of the island?"

"Let's walk around it without stopping, it won't take long."

"We won't be able to get back to land."

"It's not rising so fast, we have time enough to walk around it."

As we turned around we saw the man, standing near the boat, on the little wharf. He was looking in our direction—almost, at any rate, since he seemed rather intent on something located a bit to our left, in the midst of the swirling foam.

We went back toward him, and before we had spoken one word to him, he said:

"You want to get across."

It was not a question; without waiting for an answer he got down into the boat. We took our places in it too, as best we could. There was barely enough room for the three of us and the man, who rowed facing forward. He should have sat facing us, but he had chosen to sit in the same direction as we had, facing the prow, which required him to row backwards, in a rather awkward fashion.

At this short distance from the jetty the swells were still strong. To fight against the current the man had to give to his efforts—and to his boat—a very oblique angle with respect to the line of movement over the water. In spite of his vigorous rowing, we were moving even so at no more than a ridiculous pace. It even seemed to us, after a time, that all his energy was being spent merely to keep us motionless at the same place.

Legrand said something well intentioned about the hard task that our imprudence had inflicted on this unfortunate man; there was no response. Thinking that the man had perhaps not heard, Franz leaned forward to ask if it were really no longer possible to ford the strait on foot. There was no response to this question, either. The sailor must be deaf. He continued to row with the regularity of a machine, smoothly and without changing his course by a single degree, as if he were trying to reach, instead of the wooden wharf on the opposite shore which matched the one from which we had left, some raging part of the sea more toward the north, near where the jetty began, at the spot where a great pile of rocks lay against the brush-covered embankment, beyond which lay the end of the gradually sloping road and its two little white houses, the abrupt bend protected by the low wall, the stone roadway of the jetty stained with mossy spots, the water as calm as that of a pond, with its tufts of seaweed protruding into the water here and there and its lines of gray dust, twisting imperceptibly into spirals.

(1954)

SCENE

As the curtain opens, the first thing seen from the orchestra pit—between the sections of red velvet drawing slowly apart—the first thing glimpsed is an actor, with back turned, sitting at a worktable in the center of the brightly lighted stage.

The personage sits motionless, elbows and forearms resting on the table top. The head is turned toward the right—at about forty-five degrees—not enough to allow the features of the face to be discerned, except for the beginnings of an invisible profile: the cheek, the temple, the edge of the jaw, the outline of the ear. . . .

Nor can the hands be seen, although the attitude allows their relative position to be inferred: the left spread out flat on scattered sheets of paper, the other grasping a pen, lifted above an interrupted text for a moment of reflection. On either side are piled up in disorder a number of large books, whose shape and size would indicate them to be dictionaries—of a foreign language, no doubt—an ancient language, probably.

The head, turned toward the right, is raised: the

31

glance has moved up from the books and the interrupted sentence. It is directed toward the back of the room, to the spot where heavy, red velvet curtains conceal, from floor to ceiling, some large bay window. The folds of the curtains are vertical and very regular, at close intervals, creating, in between, deep hollows of darkness. . . .

A violent noise attracts attention to the other end of the room: blows struck against a wooden panel, so loudly and insistently as to imply that they are now being repeated, at least for the second time.

Yet the individual remains silent and motionless. Then, with no movement of the bust, the head turns, slowly, toward the left. The raised glance thus traverses the whole wall which forms the back of the large room, a wall bare—that is, without furniture—but covered with dark wood paneling, from the red curtains of the window to the panel of the closed door, which is of ordinary, or slightly less than ordinary, height. There the glance stops, while the blows at that point sound loudly again, blows so violent that the wooden panel seems to tremble.

The features of the face remain invisible, in spite of this change of posture. In fact, after a rotation of about ninety degrees, the head now occupies a position symmetrical to that of the beginning, with respect to a common central axis through the room, the table, and the chair. Thus, of an invisible profile, we can discern the other cheek, the other temple, the other ear. . . .

Once more there is a knock at the door, but more feeble, like a last entreaty—or as if in hopelessness, or in a state of calm after anguish, or of lack of assurance, or in any other mood. A few seconds later, heavy steps are heard gradually growing fainter down a long corridor.

The actor again faces toward the red curtains on the right. We hear a whistle, from between the teeth: a few notes of what must be a musical phrase—some popular song or melody—but deformed, fragmentary, difficult to identify.

Then, after a minute of silent immobility, the individual looks down again at the work to be done.

The head drops. The back hunches over. The chair back is a rectangular framework, completed by two vertical bars which support, in the center, a solid square of wood. Again we hear, weaker, even more disjointed, a few measures of the melody, whistled between the teeth.

Suddenly the personage looks up toward the door and freezes, motionless, neck tense. The position is held for many seconds—as if eavesdropping. Yet, from the auditorium, not the slightest noise can be heard.

The actor rises cautiously, pushes aside the chair without allowing it to drag or strike against the floor, and begins to walk silently toward the velvet curtains. Gently drawing forward the outer edge, on the right side, the personage looks out the window in the direction of the door—to the left. The left profile would then be discernible, if it were not hidden by the edge of red curtain held against the cheek. On the other hand, the sheets of white paper may now be seen spread out on the table.

There are a number of them, lying partially one over the other. The lower sheets, whose corners protrude on all sides in very irregular fashion, are crosshatched by closely written lines, in a very careful hand. The top sheet, the only one fully visible, is as yet only half covered with writing. The words end in the middle of a line, in an interrupted sentence, with no sign of punctuation after the last word.

From below the right edge of this sheet extends the corner of the sheet beneath: an elongated triangle, whose base measures about an inch and whose sharp point is directed toward the back part of the table, where the dictionaries are.

Still farther to the right, beyond this little point, but turned toward the side of the table, the corner of another page extends a whole hand's breadth; it, too, has a triangular form, this time close to that of a half square, cut along a diagonal. Between the peak of this last triangle and the nearest dictionary there lies, on the waxed wood of the table, a whitish object the size of a fist: a piece of rock polished by handling, hollowed out into a sort of thick cup—the thickness much greater than the depth of the cup—with irregular, rounded contours. In the bottom of the cuplike depression, a cigarette butt lies crushed out in its ashes. At the unburned end, the paper shows obvious traces of lipstick.

The actor present upon the stage, however, was—apparently—a man: hair cut short, coat and trousers. Looking up, we observe that the figure is now standing before the door, looking at it, that is, still facing away from the auditorium. From this attitude we would deduce that the actor is trying to overhear something, something going on beyond the panel of the door.

But no noise reaches the auditorium. Without turning about, the actor walks backward downstage, continuing to watch the door. From a position near the table, the right hand is placed on one corner of it and . . .

"More slowly!" a voice, at that instant, calls out from the orchestra pit. It is someone speaking through a megaphone, no doubt, since the syllables ring out with abnormal volume.

The actor stops. The voice again says:

"More slowly! Do that movement more slowly! Take it again from the door: take one step backward first—just one step—and then don't move for fifteen or twenty seconds. Then start your backward walk to the table, but much more slowly."

So the actor is again standing opposite the door, facing it, that is, still facing away from the hall. From that posture we deduce that the personage is trying to overhear something going on beyond the door. No noise reaches the auditorium. Without looking around, the actor takes one step back and again stands motionless. After a pause the figure again walks backward toward the table, where the work lies waiting, very slowly, with tiny, regularly spaced steps, while continuing to stare at the door. The motion is linear, and at constant speed. Above the legs which scarcely seem to move, the bust remains perfectly rigid, as do the two arms, held slightly apart from the body, and arched.

Reaching the vicinity of the table, the actor puts one hand—the right—on one corner, and, in order to move along the left edge, changes direction to a slight degree. Using the wooden edge as a guide, the personage moves—now, perpendicularly to the footlights . . . then, turning the corner, parallel to them . . . and sits down again on the chair, hiding with a wide back the sheets of paper spread out on the table.

The actor looks at the sheets of paper, then at the red curtains over the window, then again at the door; and, head turned in that direction, utters four or five indistinct words.

"Louder!" calls out the megaphone in the auditorium.

"And now, in this place, my life, once more . . ." says a voice of normal pitch, the voice of the actor on the stage.

"Louder!" the megaphone calls.

"And now, in this place, my life, once more . . ." the actor repeats, in a louder tone.

Then the person on the stage is again immersed in the work to be done.

(1955)

THE SHORE

Three children are walking along a beach. They walk side by side, holding each other by the hand. They are about the same height, and probably the same age: about twelve. The one in the center, nevertheless, is slightly shorter than the other two.

Except for these three children, the long shore is empty. The band of sand is fairly wide, unbroken, free of scattered rocks and water holes, sloping gently from the steep cliff, which seems unending, to the sea.

The weather is fine. The sun illuminates the yellow sand with a violent, vertical light. There is not a single cloud in the sky. Nor is there any wind. The water is blue, calm, without a trace of a swell coming in from the distance, although the beach faces the open sea and the horizon.

But at regular intervals, a quick wave, always the same, originating a few yards from the shore, suddenly rises and immediately breaks, always along the same line. The water does not seem to move forward, and then rush back; it is rather as if the whole movement occurred in a stationary position. The swelling of the water produces first a shallow trough, along the side next to the shore, and the wave draws back slightly, with a rustling noise of gravel rolling; then it bursts and spreads milkily over the slope of the beach's edge, but only to recover the space which it had lost. At most, a stronger surge rises, here and there, to moisten, for a moment, a few extra inches of sand.

And all is again motionless, the sea, flat and blue, stationary at precisely the same height on the yellow sand of the beach, on which the three children walk side by side.

They are blond, and almost the same color as the sand: their skin a little darker, their hair a little lighter. All three are dressed in the same way, short trousers and sleeveless shirts, both of a faded thick blue cloth. They are walking side by side, holding each other by the hand, in a straight line, parallel to the sea and parallel to the cliff, almost equidistant between the two, yet a little closer to the water. The sun, now at the zenith, throws no shadow at their feet.

In front of them the sand is absolutely unmarked, yellow and smooth from the rock cliff to the water. The children walk forward in a straight line, at a constant pace, without the slightest movement to either side, calmly and holding each other by the hand. Behind them the sand, barely damp, is marked by three lines of footprints left by their bare feet, three regular series of similar and equally spaced prints, clearly hollowed out, and without a seam.

The children look straight ahead. They never glance at the high cliff, on their left, or at the sea, with its little waves breaking periodically, in the other direction. Nor, even more certainly, do they turn around to look behind them at the space which they have covered. They continue on their way with a rapid and uniform step.

In front of them, a flock of sea birds walk briskly along the shore, just at the edge of the waves. They move parallel with the children, in the same direction, about a hundred yards farther on. But, as the birds do not move as fast as they, the children gain upon them. And while the sea constantly wipes out the starry tracks of the birds, the children's footsteps remain clearly inscribed in the barely damp sand, in which the three lines of footsteps grow longer and longer.

The depth of these footprints is unchanging: a little less than an inch. They are not deformed either by a crumbling of the edges or by an excessively deep impression of the heel, or of the toe. They appear as if punched out by machine in an upper, and more malleable, crust of the beach.

Thus their triple line extends, always farther, and seems at the same time to grow narrower, to slow down, to blend into a single line, which separates the beach into two bands, throughout its length, and which comes to an end in a tiny mechanical movement, far off, occurring as if in a stationary position: the alternate lifting and setting down of six bare feet.

But as the bare feet move farther along, they gain

upon the birds. Not only do they cover the ground rapidly, but the relative distance which separates the two groups diminishes even faster, compared with the space already covered. Soon there is only the gap of a few steps between them. . . .

But, when the children finally seem about to catch up with the birds, there is a flapping of wings as the birds take flight, first one, then two, then ten. . . . And the whole flock, white and gray, describes a curve above the sea as it returns to light upon the sand and begins to walk quickly again, always in the same direction, just at the edge of the waves, about a hundred yards farther on.

At this distance, the movements of the water are almost imperceptible, except for a sudden change in color, every ten seconds, at the moment when the dazzling foam shines in the sunlight.

Heedless of the footprints that they continue to press so precisely into the bare sand, indifferent to the little waves on their right, to the birds—now flying, now walking—that advance before them, the three blond children walk along side by side, with a rapid and uniform step, holding each other by the hand.

Their three sunburned faces, darker than their hair, look alike. They have the same expression: serious, thoughtful, perhaps concerned. Their features are also identical, although, obviously, two of the children are boys and the third a girl. The girl's hair is just a little longer, a little bit more curly, and her limbs appear a shade more slender. But her clothes are exactly the

same: short trousers and sleeveless shirt, both of a
faded thick blue cloth.

The girl is at the far right, next to the sea. At her
left walks the boy who is slightly less tall. The other
boy, nearest the cliff, is as tall as the girl.

Before them extends the smooth, unbroken sand, as
far as the eye can see. On their left rises the wall of
brown rock, almost vertical, and seemingly unending.
On their right, motionless and blue out to the horizon,
is the flat surface of the water, bordered by a sudden
hem, which immediately bursts and spreads out in
white foam.

Then, ten seconds later, the wave which wells up
hollows out again the same shallow trough, on the side
next to the beach, with a rustling noise of gravel rolling.

The tiny wave unfurls; the milky foam again climbs
up the slope of sand, recovering the few inches of lost
space. During the silence that follows, the tolling of a
bell, from very far away, reverberates dimly in the
quiet air.

"There's the bell," says the smallest of the children,
the boy who is walking in the middle.

But the noise of the gravel sucked in by the sea muf-
fles the weak echoes of the bell. Only at the end of the
wave cycle can a few sounds, distorted by the distance,
be heard again.

"It's the first bell," says the tall boy.

The tiny wave unfurls, on their right.

When silence returns, they hear nothing further. The
three blond children still walk at the same regular pace,

holding each other by the hand. In front of them the flock of birds, only a few steps away, is suddenly overcome by a contagious excitement. The birds flap their wings and fly upward.

They describe the same curve above the sea, and return to light upon the sand and begin to walk quickly again, always in the same direction, just at the edge of the waves, about a hundred yards farther on.

"Maybe it isn't the first," says the small boy, "maybe we didn't hear the other one, before. . . ."

"We would have heard it the same as this one," the tall boy answers.

The children have not in any way changed their pace; and the same footprints, behind them, continue to appear, as they walk forward, under the six bare feet.

"We weren't as near before," says the girl.

After a moment, the taller of the two boys, the one next to the cliff, says:

"We still aren't near."

And all three walk on in silence.

They remain silent thus until the bell, still just as faint, sounds again in the quiet air. The taller of the boys says then, "There's the bell." The others make no answer.

The birds, as the children are about to overtake them, flap their wings and fly upward, first one, then two, then ten. . . .

Then the whole flock is again back upon the sand,

moving along the shore, about a hundred yards ahead of the children.

The sea continually wipes out the starry tracks left by their feet. The children, on the other hand, who are walking closer to the cliff, side by side, holding each other by the hand, leave behind them deep prints, in a triple line which stretches out parallel to the seashore, down the long beach.

On the right, near the edge of the motionless, flat water, and always at the same spot, the same small wave wells up and breaks.

(1956)

IN THE CORRIDORS
OF THE MÉTRO

The Escalator

A group, motionless, at the bottom of the long iron-gray escalator, whose steps flatten out one after the other, at the level of the top platform, disappearing one by one with a noise of well-oiled machinery, with a heavy regularity nevertheless, and at the same time jerky, that produces an impression of unusual velocity at the place where the steps disappear one after the other beneath the horizontal surface, but which seem on the contrary to be moving extremely slowly, and without any sudden jerks, to the glance which, moving down the successive steps, again discovers at the bottom of the long, rectilinear escalator, as if still at the same spot, the identical group whose posture has not varied even slightly, a motionless group, standing on the bottommost steps, having barely left the bottom platform, has suddenly become frozen for the duration of the mechanical ascent, has come to a stop suddenly, in the midst of its agitation, of its haste, as if the act of stepping on the moving stairs had immediately paralyzed their bodies, one after the other, in poses simultaneously relaxed and stiff, suspended, marking a temporary halt in an interrupted race, while the length of the escalator continues its rise, in a regular, uniform movement, rectilinear, slow, almost imperceptible, obliquely tilted to the line of the vertical bodies.

There are five bodies, occupying three or four adjacent steps, on the left side of the stairs, more or less close to the handrail, which moves along—it also—sharing the same movement now made even less perceptible, even more doubtful, by the form of the handrail, a simple, thick ribbon of black rubber, with an unbroken surface, with two straight edges, on which no identifiable mark allows its speed to be determined, except for the two hands resting on it, about a yard apart, toward the bottom of the narrow, slanting band which everywhere else seems stationary, two hands moving upward regularly, without a jerk, synchronously with the whole system.

The uppermost of these two hands belongs to a man wearing a gray suit, of a gray that seems pale, uncertain, yellowish in the yellow light, standing alone on one step, at the top of the group, his body quite straight, his legs together, his left arm held close to his chest, his left hand holding a newspaper folded twice, over which his face leans in a position that looks somewhat exaggerated, so sharply is his neck bent forward, and whose main effect is to expose clearly, instead of his forehead and nose, the extensive bald area of the top of his head, a large round area of pink, shiny scalp across which runs, glued to the skin, a thin, wavy strand of reddish hair.

But the face suddenly looks up, toward the top of

the escalator, displaying the forehead, the nose, the mouth in an expressionless array, and remains thus several moments, longer certainly than would be necessary to be sure that the ascent, still not terminated, allows the reading of the newspaper article to be continued, as the man finally decides may be done, abruptly lowering his head, without his face, again hidden now, having revealed by the slightest sign what kind of interest he might have had in his surroundings, which indeed may not even have been observed by those two wide-open, staring eyes, with their empty look. Where the face was, in the same position as at the outset, the round skull appears, with its bald zone in the middle.

As if the man, in the midst of the reading that he has resumed, suddenly thought of that long, empty stairway, perfectly straight, that he so recently contemplated without seeing, and as if he wished by a sort of reflex, or delayed response, also to look backward, to see whether a similar empty space extended in that direction, he turns around, as abruptly as he had raised his face instants before, and without moving the rest of his body. He can observe thus that four persons are standing behind him, motionless, rising smoothly at the same speed as his own, and he immediately resumes his original position, reading his newspaper. The other passengers have not stirred.

Two steps below, after one empty step, are a woman and a child. The woman is positioned exactly behind the man with the newspaper, but she has not placed her right hand on the rail: her arm hangs beside her body, holding some handbag, or grocery sack, or roundish package whose brown bulk barely extends beyond the man's gray pants on one side, thus preventing its exact nature to be determined. The woman is neither old nor young; her face looks tired. She is wearing a red raincoat and a varicolored scarf knotted under her chin. At her left the child, a boy about ten years old wearing a turtleneck sweater and tight pants of blue denim, stands with his head half hanging down on his shoulder, his face turned upward to the right, toward the woman's profile, or else, slightly in front of it, toward the bare wall, uniformly covered with little rectangular tiles of white ceramic, that passes by with absolute regularity above the handrail, between the woman and the man with the newspaper.

There follow, always at the same speed, against this brilliant, white background cut into innumerable little rectangles, all identical and placed in orderly rows with continuous horizontal joints and alternating vertical joints, two silhouettes of men wearing dark-colored suits, the first standing behind the woman dressed in the red raincoat, two steps lower down, keeping his right hand on the rail, then, after three empty steps, the second, standing behind the child, his head hardly rising higher than the boy's thonged sandals, that is, a little below his knees, marked in the back of the blue pants by a multitude of horizontal wrinkles in the cloth.

And the rigid group continues to rise, the posture of each person remaining as unchanged as his relative position in the group. But, since the man at the top had turned around to look down, the man below him, wondering no doubt about the object of this abnormal attention, turns around also. He sees only the long series of steps leading down, and, at the very bottom of the straight, iron-gray escalator, a motionless group, standing on the bottommost steps, having just left the bottom platform, and which now rises with the same slow, sure movement, and remains constantly at the same, fixed distance.

A Corridor

A not too dense crowd of people in a hurry, all walking at the same speed, is traveling down a corridor that has no side passages, running between two elbow turns whose obtuse arcs completely hide the final exits, and whose walls are adorned, on the right as well as on the left, by identical advertising posters following each other at equal intervals. The posters display a woman's head, almost as high by itself alone as one of the people of normal height who pass in front of it, walking quickly, without a side glance.

This giant face, with its tightly curled blond hair, its eyes surrounded by very long lashes, its red lips, its white teeth, is shown in a three-quarter pose, smiling as it looks at the passers-by hurrying past one after the other, while beside it, on the left, a bottle of carbonated pop, at a forty-five-degree angle, points its opening at the partially opened mouth. The advertising slogan is written in cursive letters, in two lines: the word "even" placed above the bottle, and the word "purer" below, at the bottom of the sign, on a line that slants upward slightly from the horizontal lower edge of the poster.

The same words are found in the same place on the following poster, with the same tilted bottle whose contents are ready to spill out, and the same impersonal smile. Then, after an empty space covered with white ceramic tile, the same scene again, frozen at the same moment when the lips approach the top of the bottle held forward and the liquid contents about to gush forth, in front of which the same hurrying crowd passes by without turning a head, moving along toward the next poster.

And the mouths multiply, as do the bottles and the eyes as large as hands in the midst of their long, curving lashes. And, on the other wall of the corridor, the same features are exactly repeated (with this difference, that the directions of the glance and the bottle are reversed), following each other at constant intervals on the other side of the dark silhouettes of the travelers, who continue to move by, in a scattered but uninterrupted order, against the sky-blue background of the posters, between the reddish bottles and the pink faces with their parted lips. But, just before the elbow turn at the end of the straight corridor, the crowd is slowed down by a man who has stopped, about a yard away from the left wall. The man has on a gray suit, somewhat worn from wear, and is holding in his right hand, which hangs down alongside his body, a newspaper folded twice. He is engaged in staring at the wall, in the vicinity of a nose, bigger than his whole face, which is located level with his own eyes.

In spite of the great size of the drawing and the lack of details in its execution, the observer's head is bent forward, as if to see more clearly. The passers-by have to move aside momentarily from their straight trajectory in order to get around this unexpected obstacle; almost all pass behind the man, but some, noticing too late the scrutiny that they are about to interrupt, or not willing to change their course for such a minor matter, or aware of nothing at all, pass between the man and the poster, cutting straight through the glance.

Behind the Automatic Door

The crowd has come to a stop behind a double automatic door, now closed, that prevents access to the station platform. The stairs leading down to this area are completely full of bodies pressed one against the other, so that only the heads are visible, with few spaces between them. All the heads are motionless. The faces are frozen, showing no expression of annoyance, impatience, or hope.

Behind the frizzled expanse of the heads, men's heads for the most part, without hats, with short hair and protruding ears, and which slopes downward following the angle of the stairs, but without allowing the regularity of the steps to be perceived, rises the upper portion of the automatic doors, extending a foot or more above the closest row of heads. The two portions of the doors, closed, allow only a tiny space between, almost imperceptible. They are attached, one on the right and the other on the left, to two very straight, narrow members from which they pivot outward when opened. But, for the time being, these two pivots and the two sections of the automatic doors form a practically continuous wall which blocks all passage, rising from the level of the bottommost step.

The whole door system is painted dark green, each of the two sections bearing a big white sign against a rectangular red background, covering almost the entire width. Only the top line of the sign, "Automatic Door," is higher than the last row of heads, which allow only isolated letters of the next line to be glimpsed among the ears of the crowd.

The tightly packed heads slanting gently down the stair slope, the words "Automatic Door" twice repeated across the corridor, then, above, a horizontal band of dark green lacquer. . . . Still higher, the space is free again, up to the semicircular vault overhead, which connects the ceiling of the stairway to that of the station proper, prolonging the former to its extremity.

In this semicircular opening appears thus a part of the train platform, very small in area, and, higher up on the left, in the form of a segment of a circle sub-tended by the oblique chord formed by the edge of the platform, an even smaller fragment of one car of the train now stopped alongside the platform.

It is the side of a car made of green sheet-iron, no doubt at the very end of the train, after the last door-way, in front of which the travelers are waiting to push into the interior. Something is probably preventing them from entering as quickly as they would like—passengers getting off, or too many people inside—for they remain almost immobile, as far as one can judge by the thin margin of the crowd lying within the field of view.

The only visible elements, in fact, above the hair of the heads and the inscription at the top of the closed automatic doors, are the shoes and the trouser bottoms of the men waiting to get on the train, cut off below the knee by the circular vault of the ceiling.

The trousers are dark in color. The shoes are black, dusty. From time to time, one of them makes an upward movement, then returns to the floor, having moved forward scarcely half an inch, or not at all, or even having moved slightly backward. The nearby shoes, in front and in back, perform, next, similar movements, whose results are as imperceptible. And everything comes to rest again. Lower down, also motionless, after the band of painted metal bearing the words "Automatic Door," come the heads with their close-cut hair, their protruding ears, their expressionless faces.

(1959)

THE SECRET ROOM

To Gustave Moreau

The first thing to be seen is a red stain, of a deep, dark, shiny red, with almost black shadows. It is in the form of an irregular rosette, sharply outlined, extending in several directions in wide outflows of unequal length, dividing and dwindling afterward into single sinuous streaks. The whole stands out against a smooth, pale surface, round in shape, at once dull and pearly, a hemisphere joined by gentle curves to an expanse of the same pale color—white darkened by the shadowy quality of the place: a dungeon, a sunken room, or a cathedral—glowing with a diffused brilliance in the semidarkness.

Farther back, the space is filled with the cylindrical trunks of columns, repeated with progressive vagueness in their retreat toward the beginning of a vast stone stairway, turning slightly as it rises, growing narrower and narrower as it approaches the high vaults where it disappears.

The whole setting is empty, stairway and colonnades. Alone, in the foreground, the stretched-out body gleams feebly, marked with the red stain—a white body whose full, supple flesh can be sensed, fragile, no doubt, and vulnerable. Alongside the bloody hemisphere another identical round form, this one intact, is seen at almost the same angle of view; but the haloed point at its summit, of darker tint, is in this case quite recognizable, whereas the other one is entirely destroyed, or at least covered by the wound.

In the background, near the top of the stairway, a black silhouette is seen fleeing, a man wrapped in a long, floating cape, ascending the last steps without turning around, his deed accomplished. A thin smoke rises in twisting scrolls from a sort of incense burner placed on a high stand of ironwork with a silvery glint. Nearby lies the milkwhite body, with wide streaks of blood running from the left breast, along the flank and on the hip.

It is a fully rounded woman's body, but not heavy, completely nude, lying on its back, the bust raised up somewhat by thick cushions thrown down on the floor, which is covered with Oriental rugs. The waist is very narrow, the neck long and thin, curved to one side, the head thrown back into a darker area where, even so, the facial features may be discerned, the partly opened mouth, the wide-staring eyes, shining with a fixed brilliance, and the mass of long, black hair spread out in a complicated wavy disorder over a heavily folded cloth, of velvet perhaps, on which also rest the arm and shoulder.

It is a uniformly colored velvet of dark purple, or

which seems so in this lighting. But purple, brown, blue also seem to dominate in the colors of the cushions —only a small portion of which is hidden beneath the velvet cloth, and which protrude noticeably, lower down, beneath the bust and waist—as well as in the Oriental patterns of the rugs on the floor. Farther on, these same colors are picked up again in the stone of the paving and the columns, the vaulted archways, the stairs, and the less discernible surfaces that disappear into the farthest reaches of the room.

The dimensions of this room are difficult to determine exactly; the body of the young sacrificial victim seems at first glance to occupy a substantial portion of it, but the vast size of the stairway leading down to it would imply rather that this is not the whole room, whose considerable space must in reality extend all around, right and left, as it does toward the faraway browns and blues among the columns standing in line, in every direction, perhaps toward other sofas, thick carpets, piles of cushions and fabrics, other tortured bodies, other incense burners.

It is also difficult to say where the light comes from. No clue, on the columns or on the floor, suggests the direction of the rays. Nor is any window or torch visible. The milkwhite body itself seems to light the scene, with its full breasts, the curve of its thighs, the rounded belly, the full buttocks, the stretched-out legs, widely spread, and the black tuft of the exposed sex, provocative, proffered, useless now.

The man has already moved several steps back. He is now on the first steps of the stairs, ready to go up. The bottom steps are wide and deep, like the steps leading up to some great building, a temple or theater; they grow smaller as they ascend, and at the same time describe a wide, helical curve, so gradually that the stairway has not yet made a half-turn by the time it disappears near the top of the vaults, reduced then to a steep, narrow flight of steps without handrail, vaguely outlined, moreover, in the thickening darkness beyond.

But the man does not look in this direction, where his movement nonetheless carries him; his left foot on the second step and his right foot already touching the third, with his knee bent, he has turned around to look at the spectacle for one last time. The long, floating cape thrown hastily over his shoulders, clasped in one hand at his waist, has been whirled around by the rapid circular motion that has just caused his head and chest to turn in the opposite direction, and a corner of the cloth remains suspended in the air as if blown by a gust of wind; this corner, twisting around upon itself in the form of a loose S, reveals the red silk lining with its gold embroidery.

The man's features are impassive, but tense, as if in expectation—or perhaps fear—of some sudden event, or surveying with one last glance the total immobility of the scene. Though he is looking backward, his whole body is turned slightly forward, as if he were continuing up the stairs. His right arm—not the one holding the edge of the cape—is bent sharply toward the left, toward a point in space where the balustrade should be, if this stairway had one, an interrupted gesture, almost incomprehensible, unless it arose from an instinctive movement to grasp the absent support.

As to the direction of his glance, it is certainly aimed

at the body of the victim lying on the cushions, its extended members stretched out in the form of a cross, its bust raised up, its head thrown back. But the face is perhaps hidden from the man's eyes by one of the columns, standing at the foot of the stairs. The young woman's right hand touches the floor just at the foot of this column. The fragile wrist is encircled by an iron bracelet. The arm is almost in darkness, only the hand receiving enough light to make the thin, outspread fingers clearly visible against the circular protrusion at the base of the stone column. A black metal chain running around the column passes through a ring affixed to the bracelet, binding the wrist tightly to the column.

At the top of the arm a rounded shoulder, raised up by the cushions, also stands out well lighted, as well as the neck, the throat, and the other shoulder, the arm-pit with its soft hair, the left arm likewise pulled back with its wrist bound in the same manner to the base of another column, in the extreme foreground; here the iron bracelet and the chain are fully displayed, repre-sented with perfect clarity down to the slightest details.

The same is true, still in the foreground but at the other side, for a similar chain, but not quite as thick, wound directly around the ankle, running twice around the column and terminating in a heavy iron ring em-bedded in the floor. About a yard farther back, or perhaps slightly farther, the right foot is identically chained. But it is the left foot, and its chain, that are the most minutely depicted.

The foot is small, delicate, finely modeled. In several places the chain has broken the skin, causing notice-able if not extensive depressions in the flesh. The chain links are oval, thick, the size of an eye. The ring in the floor resembles those used to attach horses; it lies almost touching the stone pavement to which it is riveted by a massive iron peg. A few inches away is the edge of a rug; it is grossly wrinkled at this point, doubtless as a result of the convulsive, but necessarily very restricted, movements of the victim attempting to struggle.

The man is still standing about a yard away, half leaning over her. He looks at her face, seen upside down, her dark eyes made larger by their surrounding eyeshadow, her mouth wide open as if screaming. The man's posture allows his face to be seen only in a vague profile, but one senses in it a violent exaltation, despite the rigid attitude, the silence, the immobility. His back is slightly arched. His left hand, the only one visible, holds up at some distance from the body a piece of cloth, some dark-colored piece of clothing, which drags on the carpet, and which must be the long cape with its gold-embroidered lining.

This immense silhouette hides most of the bare flesh over which the red stain, spreading from the globe of the breast, runs in long rivulets that branch out, growing narrower, upon the pale background of the bust and the flank. One thread has reached the armpit and runs in an almost straight, thin line along the arm; others have run down toward the waist and traced out, along one side of the belly, the hip, the top of the thigh, a more random network already starting to congeal. Three or four tiny veins have reached the hollow between the legs, meeting in a sinuous line, touching the point of the V formed by the outspread legs, and disappearing into the black tuft.

Look, now the flesh is still intact: the black tuft and the white belly, the soft curve of the hips, the narrow waist, and, higher up, the pearly breasts rising and falling in time with the rapid breathing, whose rhythm grows more accelerated. The man, close to her, one knee on the floor, leans farther over. The head, with its long, curly hair, which alone is free to move somewhat, turns from side to side, struggling; finally the woman's mouth twists open, while the flesh is torn open, the blood spurts out over the tender skin, stretched tight, the carefully shadowed eyes grow abnormally larger, the mouth opens wider, the head twists violently, one last time, from right to left, then more gently, to fall back finally and become still, amid the mass of black hair spread out on the velvet.

At the very top of the stone stairway, the little door has opened, allowing a yellowish but sustained shaft of light to enter, against which stands out the dark silhouette of the man wrapped in his long cloak. He has but to climb a few more steps to reach the threshold.

Afterward, the whole setting is empty, the enormous room with its purple shadows and its stone columns proliferating in all directions, the monumental staircase with no handrail that twists upward, growing narrower and vaguer as it rises into the darkness, toward the top of the vaults where it disappears.

Near the body, whose wound has stiffened, whose brilliance is already growing dim, the thin smoke from the incense burner traces complicated scrolls in the still air: first a coil turned horizontally to the left, which then straightens out and rises slightly, then returns to the axis of its point of origin, which it crosses as it moves to the right, then turns back in the first direction, only to wind back again, thus forming an irregular sinusoidal curve, more and more flattened out, and rising, vertically, toward the top of the canvas.

(1962)